Loves
Deception

By

Nicole Y Moore

This book is dedicated to my loving husband, three wonderful children, and supportive family and friends.

To you, the reader, I wanted to give you something edgy mixed with a sense of realism. My word choice was on purpose, sometimes a spade is a spade. I hope you're not offended or find it vulgar. You're about to read a book of which, I deliciously agonized over. I enjoyed writing it and hope you will enjoy reading it.

Be on the lookout for its sequel.

Contents

Chapter 1

Gianna woke from a dream that had good potential but turned into a mix of emotions. It started with a tall dark and handsome man escorting her through a crowded restaurant. When they reached their table he pulled out her chair and helped her get seated. The waiter came to take their order and before she could speak tall dark and handsome had selected her favorite meal and choice of wine. Gianna was so impressed that she looked up but could only see a dark shadow where his face should've been.

Spooked by this Gianna stood knocking over her water goblet spilling its contents all over the beautiful table.

Tall dark and handsome appeared by her side to help calm her nerves. His touch on her shoulder and lower back sent electric shivers all down her spine causing her legs to weaken. The need to lean into him for support was strong. His touch felt familiar and right.

Gianna looked up at tall dark and handsome and without seeing him she felt somehow she knew him. She felt safe and protected in his arms. Swept up in the moment Gianna leaned in to kiss him but before their lips met, tall dark and handsome disappeared.

Gianna lay in bed trying to figure out how a missed kiss from a familiar stranger in a dream could cause so many emotions. Her mind drifting to what the kiss would have felt like and how the familiar stranger's hands would have touched her body. Forgetting herself Gianna began to surrender her dream to reality. Her hands began to roam all over her body resting in the valley of her pleasure. She began to imagine her hands were his and that they were alone and ready for each other. She stroked and played with herself until she was so close to sweet release. Just as her wave of pleasure took her she heard someone call her name.

Bryan entered the house wondering what Gianna would be cooking. Every Saturday morning like clockwork Bryan would come over and they would have breakfast and swap Friday date night stories.

He put his things down by the door and put his keys in the bowl on the table. He looked around the foyer and noticed Gianna's keys next to his and her purse on the bench. He remembered the time they made the bench from scratch. Gianna needed a distraction, Kevin had gone on another "business trip" without her. They worked on the bench all night and drank way too much wine.

He touched the side of the bench where the effects of too much alcohol began to show. Stained finger prints on the bench seemed like a brilliant idea at the time. To this day Gianna maintains that it adds character and symbolizes their longtime friendship. Bryan looked down at his fingertips and remembered how long it took to get the stain off their hands.

Laughing to himself, Bryan left the foyer and entering the kitchen he found it empty and without the familiar smell of breakfast cooking. He figured Gianna must still be sleeping. He thought about checking in on her but decided to make her breakfast in bed. Bryan rarely got a chance to show off his cooking skills. Having spent 4 years studying under the world renowned Chef Grey, Bryan knew his way around a kitchen.

Crossing the expansive modern marble floors to the glass cabinets, he pulled out several pots and pans. He gathered the ingredients for pancakes, a Spanish style omelet, and Gianna's favorite, pork roll. He grabbed several oranges for fresh squeezed orange juice and added a little pineapple juice to it. Finishing up the last pancake and plating the eggs he decided to make sure Gianna was still sleeping.

Bryan made his way up the back stairs and down the hall to Gianna's room. Gianna's door at the end of the hall was slightly ajar. He moved quietly so he didn't wake her. As Bryan moved closer he heard rustling and noises that he couldn't make out. Bryan began to worry that Gianna maybe having a nightmare so he walked a little faster. He wasn't sure but the noises were getting louder and the sounds were more in line with moaning.

It finally occurred to Bryan that maybe he was interrupting her with another man. For a brief moment he wondered if Kevin was back in the picture. For some reason this thought made Bryan angry. Kevin was Gianna's ex-boyfriend. He was a world class narcissist and hit on everything that moved. Gianna did the right thing dumping him. She just couldn't ever find out that Bryan kept him away. Kevin would have wormed his way in over a thousand more times if Bryan didn't step in. The more Bryan thought about it the more Bryan wondered what could have Kevin forgetting his end of the deal. Bryan made it to the door but peaked in first, in case he was wrong. "If Kevin goes back on his end of the deal I'll kill him", Bryan murmured under his breath.

Gianna was on the bed. She had her eyes closed and was moaning and writhing and thrashing about the bed.

One hand had a grip on the tan satin sheets while the other was playing with her clitoris. Bryan froze. Unable to move or look away he watched as his best friend, since the third grade, pleasured herself.

Bryan could see her sweet pussy lips and the fingers that pleasured her clitoris. Her legs were spread open and she was gyrating in sync with her fingers on her clit. Gianna began to violently rock against her fingers. She began to play with her ample breasts. She moaned louder and it was obvious her pleasure would be coming down any minute. Bryan watched unable to move as Gianna pushed two of her fingers into her sweet wet pussy.

Bryan was unsure of what to do. He couldn't look away. Gianna's curves and the rhythmic movement of her body had him paralyzed. His manhood had grown hard as a rock making him uncomfortable in his jeans. He put a hand down his jeans with the intention to adjust his cock but the very touch made it impossible to resist further contact. Bryan began to stroke himself through his boxer briefs as he watched and listened to Gianna.

The urge to go to her, remove her fingers and slide his thick and now pulsating cock in her, was slowly creeping into his mind. As Gianna's cream drenched her fingers it made Bryan wish he did just that. Bryan couldn't help himself, seeing Gianna move her fingers in and out of her pussy, and hearing her moan and groan he relieved his cock from his jeans and boxers and began to freely stroke himself. Gianna's body, his thoughts and the smell of her sex in the air led to an explosive release. Caught up in the moment Bryan called out Gianna's name.

Gianna closed her eyes tight and as she climaxed she screamed and moaned her pleasure. She climaxed harder than Kevin could have ever made her. She shook and vibrated and enjoyed the wave of pleasure that took her body. Coming down from her high, she had a strange feeling she was being watched. Regaining some composure, she looked toward her bedroom door.

Gianna sat up in her bed and looked but didn't see anything. "Who did you think would be there?" Gianna thought out loud. She kicked the covers from around her ankles and headed toward her bathroom. She looked in the mirror and instantly felt silly. "I can't believe that dream made feel me so, umm good," Gianna said to her reflection. Gianna smiled. "Well it has been awhile since you got some. I deserved that! No. I deserve tall dark and handsome from my dream." Gianna started the shower stepped in and lost herself to her thoughts under the spray of warm water.

Bryan couldn't believe what he'd just witnessed. He couldn't believe that he lost all self-control and violated his best friend's privacy like that. Bryan looked in the hall mirror steps away from Gianna's bedroom door. "What just happened? I... what was I thinking? I'm sure she didn't see me I moved just in time. But still that was close." Bryan told himself.

Bryan was jarred from his thoughts by the sound of Gianna walking to the bathroom. He froze trying not to make any sounds that would draw attention to himself. Bryan stood there frozen until he heard the shower come on. He cleaned away the evidence of his explosion and hurried down the hall to the back stairs toward the kitchen.

Bryan cleaned himself up in the powder room. Trying to put what he'd just witnessed aside he began to set two place settings for the breakfast he'd made. Trying to build up a since of normalcy he retrieved the paper from the front yard and began to read it at the kitchen table.

Gianna heard the front door open and close and knew it was Bryan, her best friend. He was on-time as usual but she was unusually late. By now, breakfast would've been on the table and they would've been swapping stories. Finishing up her shower, Gianna dressed in her yoga pants and tank top and left her wet hair to air dry. "Curls today I guess, too tired to do anything else with it."

Gianna made her bed and started down the stairs. She turned the corner and walked into the kitchen. Bryan hadn't noticed her enter the room so she stood there awhile and watched him. She couldn't remember the last Saturday they'd missed performing this morning ritual. Bryan would come over and they would fill their Saturday with gossip, watch movies and play games. The best games were thought up on the fly. They would spend Saturday like this until the sun was coming back up again. Gianna loved spending Saturday's with Bryan because no Saturday was ever the same.

He was usually busy during the week but he always managed to sneak in a few emails or text messages to Gianna throughout the day. He always read her blog and made sure to comment and share it on his social media pages. If she really felt he needed to slow down she would pop in and take him out to lunch. Saturdays were the catch up days, where the hustle and bustle was on hold.

Bryan continued to stare at the paper unable to concentrate. He couldn't get the image of Gianna on her bed completely naked and finger fucking herself off of his mind. Bryan had to get it together. He could feel his manhood stirring to life with every thought. He could hear every moan and see every curve stored in his memory. Knowing that Gianna would be down soon he didn't want to greet her with a hard dick in his jeans. He just couldn't quite shake the image of Gianna's curves and her wet fingers in her pussy. Bryan brought the paper into focus and started reading the sports page but felt himself slip off into a daydream.

Bryan and Gianna had been friends for as long as he could remember. This wasn't the first time he had seen her naked but most the recent time was at Lake Tigan. They went skinny dipping on a couples camping trip a few years back with a group of friends. Gianna and Kevin, Tracy and Bryan left the other couples at the cabin and went to the lake. They played a made up game where everyone had to jump into the lake or they would have to walk back to the cabin in the dark without a flash light. Lake Tigan's woods were scary at night so everyone knew they had to jump in. The catch was that they had to strip naked before they jumped in.

Bryan went first he wasn't shy. He took every stitch of his clothes off and paraded around the rim of the cliff before he jumped in Olympic style and transformed it into a cannon ball dive. The splash from his dive wet everyone's clothes making it harder to get off. The water was surprisingly warm so he invited everyone to jump in and get it over with.

Tracy was next to jump in. Tracy was Bryan's girlfriend at the time. They had been dating for 6 months and they were already having problems. Bryan was a good guy and he treated her like a queen but she was spoiled and needy. Bryan wasn't sure how he missed the signs, but by the end of this camping trip they would break up and make up over the course of a year and a half.

Tracy was scared. She didn't want to be seen naked and she didn't want to jump. She made every excuse not to do it. Bryan knew a full melt down was coming so he reasoned with her. He offered to have every one turn around so she felt more comfortable. This worked and scored Bryan points he cashed in when they were alone.

Tracy peeled off her wet clothes revealing her black string bikini with a little slit that barely covered her nipples. Her smooth complexion and deep brown eyes drove Bryan crazy. She worked as a designer for a major magazine and had a trained eye for fashion. Her swim suit was to be featured in the upcoming issue of her magazine. Bryan enjoyed seeing every inch of her, including the sugar and spice wrapped in diamonds tattoo on the small of her back. She jumped but it seemed like she was moving in slow motion, she perfectly breached the surface of the lake. When she came up out of the water she looked like an angel with the moonlight glistening on her skin and her wet curls framing her face.

Next up was Kevin and he went quickly thank God. He mumbled and grumbled the whole time but he did jump in. Gianna was up next and she hesitated a little. She had a polka dot pink and purple bikini underneath her cut off shorts and her tank top she folded up to show off her abs.

Gianna was proud of her six pack. Bryan and Gianna went to the gym six days a week for 3 months to prepare for this trip. We went to the lake every year around the same time but that year she brought along Kevin and Bryan brought Tracy.

Gianna began to slowly remove her tank top showing her Polka dot top and next removed her cutoffs. She created a slow tease for Kevin not caring that they weren't alone. When she got down to her bathing suit she must have remembered she had an audience because she tried to jump in with her suit on.

Tracy, a little bitter that she had to strip all the way down, reminded her of how dark the woods were at night. Kevin who was red in the face looked over at Bryan. He was a little ticked that his private strip show wasn't so private. Gianna got Tracy's hint and peeled her bikini top off. Bryan could swear her breasts bounced happy to be free. Next she took off her bikini bottoms and wiggled her booty in Kevin's direction then quickly dove in.

The water was clear and the moon beamed on the surface. Each couple spent time kissing and enjoying the mood. Tracy was a little miffed that she had to play this game with other people. Bryan tried to console her but wasn't winning the battle. He overheard Kevin telling Gianna that her body should only be for his eyes to see. Bryan looked over at Gianna in time to see her roll her eyes at Kevin. Bryan laughed which Tracy mistook for him laughing at her. She narrowly missed punching Bryan in the shoulder. Bryan sighed and locked eyes with Gianna as their respective dates nagged them endlessly. That wasn't the first time Bryan had seen Gianna naked but unlike those times, something was different.

Gianna stood in the doorway watching Bryan's 6 foot tall 190 pound frame as he read the morning paper. His smooth brown skin contrasted by his goatee, went perfectly with his light brown designer button up shirt and black jeans that brought out his light brown eyes. Bryan kept himself pretty fit. They went to the gym together and pushed each other to the max.

Gianna put her hands on her stomach thinking of how she owed her six pack to him. He was all muscle and he pushed her until she was the same. Of course Gianna had a few areas she wanted to keep tight but not hard bodied. She wanted to keep her body supple and not look like a female body builder who over did it.

Gianna took a closer look at Bryan and realized he looked more like he was day dreaming than reading the paper. She stood there awhile longer just watching, wondering what he was thinking about. After a few minutes she pushed further into the kitchen causing Bryan to look up. Gianna smiled and couldn't help but smell the fresh orange-pineapple juice and breakfast.

"Mmm, I should sleep in every Saturday morning," Gianna said while taking her seat across from Bryan.

Bryan smiled, "morning." She leaned over and kissed his cheek.

"Hey I wouldn't mind freshening up my culinary skills," Bryan answered while dishing out the omelet onto Gianna's plate. "Your just in time too, everything is nice and hot."

"You seemed to be day dreaming a minute ago. Penny for your thoughts," Gianna inquired.

"Oh I was remembering our last couple's trip to Lake Tigan," Bryan replied.

Gianna took another bite and drank some of her juice. "What made you think of our trip a year ago? We go every year, in fact the Cabin will be available to us earlier and for two extra weeks if we want it this year."

"Yeah that sounds good. You going to be okay with Kevin not being there this year?"

"Kevin? Oh Uh." Gianna nervously took a bite of her omelet. "He made his choice and now he has to live with it." Gianna didn't want to spoil the mood. She knew Bryan and Kevin only tolerated each other for her sake. She was keeping a secret from Bryan and now wasn't the time to bring it up. She changed the subject. "I seem to remember you and me starting this little tradition. So I'm fine kicking your but in our cabin games. Wait, are you bringing Tracy this year?"

"Good, just checking on you. Nah, Tracy and I broke up. We keep in touch but I'm not bringing her this time." Gathering a fork full of delicious pancakes. Bryan suddenly was in an investigative mood he decided to have a little fun. "So, did you sleep well?" Brian smirked.

Gianna paused in the middle of sipping her juice and looked at Bryan. It was a normal question to ask but it felt different. Suddenly embarrassed a flash back of her sexual escapade came to mind. Heat surged to her pussy, and her clitoris began to pulsate. She felt her nipples harden and her heart racing. She desperately hoped Bryan didn't notice that she was horny. He knew how long it'd been since she had gotten some. She did the best she could to relieve those sexual needs. However, she was craving a strong man to wrap her legs around. She wanted her pleasure to rain down around his cock instead of her fingers or her toys. Gianna simply nodded her head while fanning herself. Bryan was always good at reading her so she hoped she put on a good front.

Bryan could see that Gianna was embarrassed, she was turning red. He also knew that this morning was the first time she tried to relive her sexual tension in a while. She seemed more relaxed. "It seems she won't be letting me in on this little secret." Bryan was getting a kick out of seeing Gianna squirm. She actually looked like she needed a few minutes or she would come again. Honestly, Bryan would've put breakfast on hold just to make it happen, so he could watch.

Bryan couldn't imagine what could have caused her to cum so hard against her fingers. "Hell and make me Jerk off in the middle of the hallway looking at my best friend. She can keep this secret. I'm sure not going to tell her of my hallway peep show." Bryan thought. Nothing like that has ever happened between us. He's still in shock that any of it happened.

"Well, did you have a date last night," Bryan couldn't resist pushing the subject a little. Bryan was curious and wondered what caused this sudden need and want in Gianna.

As a man he also wondered if he stopped in earlier on their Saturday mornings would he be treated to another show like the one half hour an ago. Something in him made an immediate appointment to come earlier on Saturdays. He smiled and almost laughed out loud. He was ashamed at first but dismissed it because he was definitely tempted to find out.

Gianna's sensual moment was interrupted. "No, I stayed in last night had to come up with ideas for my blog. I thought I texted you that. Wondered why you didn't come over. Did you have a date?"

"Oh. I remember my phone going off but I didn't check it. I was avoiding Tracy. Did you come up with an idea for your blog?"

"Well you know how I have been going on dates, right? Well I decided to kind of document the ones that were just a flat out no for a second date. I need people to know why I have been single for 6 months. Someone out there will appreciate my research and not make the same mistakes."

"What are you talking about? Man, I think you are choosing to be single. There was nothing wrong with the last dates I met of yours. Ken seemed into you and he had a good job. Mike seemed like potential. I sized them up and googled them, for your protection of course, and they panned out. No records or anything. Besides my image consulting instincts say they pass the preliminary rounds."

"Well, I'm glad you're my second Daddy, out here googling people. Gianna laughed. Ken and Mike were on the better side of things but not sending me second date vibes. So, my blog will be like a dating diary. I will find Mr. Right." Gianna dipped her finger into the syrup left on her plate and licked it off her finger.

Bryan could no longer concentrate. He was trying not to think about her like that but he wanted to lick her fingers. He wished instead of syrup it was her pleasure he would be licking off her fingers. Not paying attention to what Gianna was saying, he felt his manhood start to jump. All he could think, as he watched her lick the syrup off her fingers, was of them circling her clitoris and moving in and out of her pussy. All of this happening no more than half an hour ago still had Bryan a little shook up. Bryan covered his cock with his hand to hide any evidence of what he was thinking. He tried to concentrate on what Gianna was saying.

Gianna was in the middle of a sentence but noticed a strange look in Bryan's eyes. His eyes looked dark and sensuous and he was licking his lips. Strangely this sent a delicious shiver straight to her pussy. "Oh?" she thought feeling embarrassed for the second time this morning. Gianna looked around trying to find something to concentrate on.

She noticed for the first time the amount of food and prep time it must've taken to make. Gianna started to get a sinking feeling that Bryan was around longer than when she first heard him come in. "Just how early did Bryan arrive to make all this food," she wondered. "I really hope that he didn't get here too early."

"Um, I heard you come in while I was in the shower. Were you just getting here?"

"Actually, no I was here earlier. That's why everything is ready for you to eat. I wanted to let you sleep in and I would bring breakfast to you. You're always up taking care of me. Thought it was the least I could do." Bryan looked up at Gianna. She looked like she was in deep thought. The look on her face said she wasn't going to fess up but she was starting to wonder something.

Gianna's face froze. "Could that explain the feeling I had of being watched, or thinking I heard someone call me. No, Bryan couldn't have seen anything." Gianna looked at Bryan searching his eyes, trying to see if maybe she was right. Bryan continued to stare straight into her eyes but gave no clues as to whether he'd seen anything. "Then why did it feel like you were being watched," She asked herself.

Bryan didn't push any further he had a feeling that Gianna knew what he was getting at. He also didn't want to have to explain just how long he stood outside her door. Bryan moved over to the sink and began cleaning up. Gianna walked over to him and took the dishes from his hands. "Now you know how this works, I cook you clean. This time you cooked so it's my turn to clean." Gianna brushed past Bryan and reached around him for the dish soap. Gianna tried to put it out of her mind that Bryan may have seen her. As she reached for the dish soap her breast touched his arm. Her nipples immediately hardened. She looked up and met Bryan's light brown eyes.

Bryan tensed up feeling her breast on his arm. He could see that her nipples had hardened causing his cock to become semi hard. He stared at her and looked down her delicious body. He shook it off and was disappointed in himself for his reaction. He also felt he should just come out and tell her he'd seen her upstairs. They didn't keep secrets and he didn't want things to get awkward.

Every detail of their sex life with others were explored and dissected. Gianna called it research that would only make it better next time for both of them. The difference was that neither of them witnessed each other's act. He held Gianna's gaze a little longer. This was his way of apologizing. He put a finger under her chin, tilting her head to get her full attention. "You'll find him," he said. Gianna already weak, nearly surrendered everything. "Oh um, who." Gianna couldn't help the breathless stutter. She was still affected by her dream and subsequent events. Bryan was inches from her face but moved in closer his lips graving the corner of her mouth on a path past her cheek. He whispered in her ear, "Mr. right, he's close."

Gianna eased away first as to avoid making a fool of herself. If Bryan wasn't careful he would be a part of the subsequent dream affects. His look was doing something to her, but when his closeness, ooh, she could feel it down low. She put some distance between them and continued cleaning up. She really wished she'd worn a t-shirt instead of a tank top. She knew her nipples were hard and very visible. "It's all because of that dream. That's all," she thought. She really missed the feel of strong hands holding her. Gianna's daydream was interrupted as Bryan asked her a question.

"Are you alright?" Bryan really needed to ask himself that question. He nearly kissed Gianna right then and there. Never mind that as soon as he saw her hard nipple and looked into her eyes he wanted to take her right back to that bed.

"Um, yeah! I'm just whew, stuffed. Gianna avoided eye contact keeping herself busy putting away the left overs. She knew he could tell she was lying. Why do you ask?"

"Gianna you know you can talk to me right?" Bryan was on the verge of confessing. Anything to have his daydream realized. "Best friend or not I'm a man, and she is doing things to me right now." Bryan was having trouble keeping it together.

Gianna held Bryans gaze once again. She wondered if she was being silly. They didn't have secrets. "I should just tell him about my dream and ask him what he saw. No. I.. no." Gianna quickly made up an excuse to explain her jumpy behavior. Bryan, seeing that he was being pushy, decided to drop it. Bryan was always direct but he thought this situation was different.

Bryan began to tell her about his new client for Bryan Stillwater's Image Consultant Firm. Bryan opened his own Image consultant firm roughly five years ago and has built the careers for everyone from the Palladino Saints star Quarterback Mitchell Graham to Singer/Song Writer Eli Star. Now Bryan was working with a mutual friend Charlene Stanton.

Charlene a model herself, but also owned her own modeling agency and was looking for a new fresh face for a campaign ad for Michael Yvann Cologne. Bryan was scheduled to meet her today and the news was that she would meet him at Gianna's house. They would all catch up and talk a little business at the same time.

Gianna was excited to see Charlene. It had been months since Charlene had been in town. They kept in touch by phone once a week but it wasn't the same. Gianna finished wiping down the counters and Bryan insisted on sweeping the floor. They worked together and continued to talk about his ideas for who would be perfect for one of Charlene's model.

Chapter 2

Once the kitchen was clean they moved into the family room. Bryan turned on the TV and started the search for a good movie to watch. Gianna sat in her usual spot next to Bryan. Bryan pulled the blanket from the couch and placed it over them. He gathered Gianna up in his arms and they watched Gianna's favorite, a horror movie. Gianna couldn't watch it unless she had something to cover her eyes during the really scary parts and Bryan's shoulder for back up. Bryan's job was to fill her in on what was happening during those scary parts. Bryan got a kick out of how she always picked the scariest ones but could never last past the first sign of trouble.

Gianna made herself comfortable. She snuggled up to Bryan and got her pillow ready. With one hand on his chest and the other gripping the pillow she tried to get into the movie. After a few minutes she found herself in deep thought. Giana had been keeping something from Bryan. She wasn't sure how to bring it up but she knew she had to. She was also still thinking about their encounter in the kitchen. She was admonishing herself for it. Gianna couldn't explain it but if she hadn't stepped way, reluctantly, things could have gotten out of hand.

Bryan was having trouble concentrating on the movie. His mind kept wandering back to the kitchen, and the bedroom. He tried to focus on his plans for the evening. He was excited to tell Gianna about the dinner party he had planned. He was sure she would be excited as well. He was thinking of the entertainment portion of the party. He wanted to come up with a good game to play. He was going to suggest a drinking game when Charlene got there after they discussed business. He also had a surprise for Charlene. He had the perfect model in mind for her agency. His name was Miles Thomas. He was in advertising but was perfect for the cologne ad and he was looking to break into modeling.

Miles was an old college buddy that moved to town for business. He looked Bryan up to see if he could help him with an image to help break into modeling. He should be coming over around 6:30 pm and Charlene would be there by 6pm. Perfect timing. Miles was always into something back when they were in college. There was never a dull moment with him around. Talking to him for the past few months he seemed to have slowed down considerably. He was focusing on his career and was really interested in breaking into modeling. He has a pretty good shot at it too. That was good because if he gets this ad things would move fast and he needed to be ready.

The movie finally ended with Gianna's face pressed firmly into his neck. She was literally glued to him. Bryan finished telling her how it ended and Gianna slowly peeled herself away once the credits started rolling. They both busted out laughing once they made eye contact. "Why do you pick these movies only to stay glued to me, you didn't even get to see the movie?" Bryan laughed so hard he couldn't even help it. Gianna laughed too! "I love scary movies, but I can't take it. It's better when you narrate. Just come on help me clean up or put on another one."

Bryan let Gianna know of what he had planned for the evening. Gianna was cool with it. He decided to order dinner in and Gianna suggested they order from Gina's Soul Food on E 79th Street. She suggested they could pick up the food around 5:00 and be back in time for Charlene to arrive. Gianna mentioned needing to get more wine so they would stop at Vito's on the corner.

Gianna tried to broach the subject of her secret but found that this wasn't a good time. Bryan seemed so excited to have tonight go well. She didn't want to bring down his mood. Telling him that she'd been talking to Kevin Sims would definitely kill the mood. Gianna knew that Bryan felt she could do better than Kevin. He still remembers the many break up to make up days. Kevin had some growing up to do they both did.

Gianna met Kevin Sims in college. She, Charlene and a few other good girl friends were at a frat party when she locked eyes with Kevin. Kevin had on a deep blue shirt with his fraternity letters stretched over his broad muscular chest. He wore a pair of jeans and the latest basketball shoes. He was posted up next to the DJ table talking to his friends. Gianna and her girls had just walked in and was checking out the scene.

"Hey, I'm going to freshen up my makeup. I think the bathrooms over there," Charlene said. The girls followed Charlene to the bathroom.

"I can't believe we got invited, this is the biggest party of the year," Gianna said.

"Yeah, I know I thought we were going to have to go to *Whiskey's* again. You know that place is full of old heads just praying for a night with us young tenderoni's." As Charlene finished her sentence she was bumped into by a strong handsome brick wall.

"Sorry, I wasn't watching where I was going," said Michael. Michael Yvann turned around. "Oh! I wasn't expecting someone so beautiful. My name is Michael, Michael Yvann." He reached out and took Charlene's hand and kissed it. "Everyone calls me Mike."

"Thanks, Mike but you should really be more careful," Charlene said taking her hand back as she walked past him. Looking over her shoulder she could see he was still checking her out. She yelled her name over the music to him and he smiled.

The girls continued on to the bathroom. Gianna was the first to speak. "Girl I can't believe you were so rude to that fine brother"

"I wasn't rude he was. He should have been paying attention to what he was doing. Plus girl he was fine and I wanted him to remember me. Watch he will be looking for me by the end of the night." Charlene powdered her nose and adjusted her breasts in her skin tight black *"Cianni Valeris"* dress.

"Girls you better take notes. I've seen Charlene at work, she always gets her man. She is working her magic on that brother and he won't know what hit him. You just wait and see, he will be on her all night," said Shelly.

"Well I still think that you were a little harsh," said Gianna. Gianna looked herself over one more time. She wore a blue wrap dress with black strappy heels. Gianna applied red lips and touched up her makeup.

"Uh no Gianna, It's all a part of my plan," said Charlene. "Boys only want what they can't have. Once a boy gets what he wants he's gone. Men on the other hand see what they want and get it and keep it. I am just trying to figure out which one he is. Honey, I am a keeper so I need a man," Charlene said as she gave herself a wink and air kissed her reflection.

The ladies finished applying their makeup, pushed up their breasts and gave their butts a good once over before going back to the party. Gianna stood in the mirror a little longer. She replayed Charlene's answer in her mind. "Hmm that makes sense. Which do I want? Am I ready for a man? Or am I still playing with boys?" She didn't have an answer.

In the club the girls danced to every song. They were having a ball. Charlene had it right, Michael Yvann was on her all night. He had a friend for all of us. Gianna was talking to Devin, Shelly was talking to Kevin. The rest of the girls weren't interested in the other guys. They were dancing and flirting with the DJ. Devin was cute he was a little short for her taste though. He dressed right and he was smooth as a baby's bottom but there wasn't any chemistry.

Gianna looked over at Charlene and Michael and knew that they were a good fit. She looked over at Shelly and Kevin. She was shocked to see Kevin staring back at her. Their locked eyes and they held. Shelly didn't seem to notice she just kept talking. He smiled and nodded politely in the right moments but clearly didn't hear anything Shelly was saying. It was fine for Shelly she loved to talk.

Kevin had a fresh High top fade, deep penetrating brown eyes and the right body filling out the letters on his blue shirt. Kevin was more her type and her body seemed to know it too. Gianna looked away and back to Devin. Devin must have gotten the picture and asked if she wanted to join them. Once over there Devin sparked a conversation with Shelly and just like that the couples changed. They excused themselves leaving Gianna and Kevin alone. Kevin spoke first.

"Hey, I'm Kevin Sims. Your Gianna right? Yeah I think we have a few classes together," Kevin said.

"I'm taking some intense classes this semester. I barely have time to look at anything but the board. Which classes are we in together?" Gianna was impressed that Kevin noticed her. He was on the Football, Basketball and Track team and was a part of the best fraternity on campus.

"English Lit, Chemistry and Advanced Calculus. I noticed you first in English Lit. Professor Shea's class isn't too tough. Kevin didn't want to scare her but he wanted her to know he noticed her. She was smoking hot and the best part was that she didn't know it yet.

Gianna and Kevin talked and danced for hours that night. He saw her back to her dorm and kissed her until her toes curled. They went their separate ways that night but would be in separable all through college. They dated off and on after college and up until 6 months ago they were engaged. Gianna snapped out of her trip down memory lane. She got on her sweater and grabbed her keys and she and Bryan both headed out the door.

Chapter 3

Bryan and Gianna arrived back at Gianna's house having picked up the food. As planned they picked up four bottles of wine two Red, one White and one blush. They also grabbed bottles of Paul Masson Peach and Amsterdam Vodka Pineapple. Bryan thought it would be a good ice breaker to play a drinking game after business was done. Miles didn't know many people in town and Charlene was just getting back into town. So a drinking game would be a good way to loosen up the mood.

Bryan was upstairs in the guest bedroom getting ready for dinner. He kept spare clothes and toiletries at Gianna's because he usually slept over every Saturday night unless they had dates or if Tracy and Kevin were in the picture. Bryan took a shower and freshened up then went to the closet.

Thinking about the meeting, he hoped Miles would impress Charlene with the pointers he'd given him. Charlene had a sharp eye and knew exactly what she wanted. She easily enticed models to switch to her agency and they went on to have better careers for it. Bryan wanted the meeting to go well so it didn't ruin the rest of the evening. He wanted everyone to be comfortable and have a relaxing time. He continued getting dressed and when he was done he went down to the kitchen and opened a bottle of wine.

Gianna decided to change into something host worthy. She had never met Miles before and hadn't seen Charlene in a month. She wanted to look good. There was something to be said for first impressions. Gianna stepped out of her closet holding a chocolate brown wrap dress and a royal blue satin button up shirt that just covered her ample bottom. She was going to pair it with her black satin leggings. Gianna's caramel complexion and dark brown eyes would go perfectly with the chocolate brown dress that hugged her curves, but she would be more comfortable in the latter.

The Royal blue button up was an impulse buy a Liam's Boutique. It was the only button up Gianna had ever seen with a low neck line that dipped to reveal the top of her breasts, ended just above her waistline in the front and reached just below her bottom in the back. The top hugged her in all the right places and was perfect for a little peek-a-boo in leggings. The leggings were smooth to the touch and so comfortable. Both outfits were dress casual and definitely fit the occasion.

Holding up both outfits against her body in the mirror Gianna decided to go with comfort. She put the dress back in her closet and changed into the latter. She added a few accessories and went with her royal blue wedges. She had to do something to her hair so she sprayed it with her homemade leave in and added a little Eco Styler gel to hold the curls and tame the fly-a-ways. Gianna played with her curls and decided to put it up in the back leaving a few tendrils to hang down in the front. She applied a little make up but added killer red lips and long lashes. She looked at herself in the mirror.

"Ooh girl how are you single?" Her eyes drifted to the bed through the mirror. Gianna remembered her dream and how tall dark and handsome seemed so familiar. She felt so comfortable with him. "I really hope he doesn't turn out to be Kevin. That would be a waste of a good dream." Gianna said to her reflection and laughed.

In the kitchen, Bryan had opened the red wine and was setting the table. After pouring two glasses he called to let Gianna know that her glass was in the kitchen. Bryan decided to call Miles to make sure he had Gianna's address.

"Hey Bryan, What's up we still on for 6:30 pm tonight?

"Yeah you ready? I wanted to make sure you got the address and you don't have any trouble finding the place."

"Yeah I programmed it into my GPS so I should find it fine. You need me to bring anything?"

"Yeah your headshots and your resume. We will discuss a little business first then we can loosen up the atmosphere and you can meet everyone on a different level."

"Alright that sounds cool. I'll call you when I'm close by. You can turn the porch light on for me or something. You sure I shouldn't bring the lady of the house anything or maybe Charlene?"

"Nah man, I got you covered. Look I'll see you in few.

"Alright man, see you."

Gianna walked into the kitchen as Bryan was finishing up a call. Gianna noticed he put on a light blue button up and a pair of dark blue jeans. She recognized them as the extra clothes he kept in the guest bedroom. Bryan filled out his shirt perfectly. His muscles were visible but not to overpowering for the look. From this angle his butt was on point in those pants.

Bryan noticing that Gianna was in the room turned around in time to see her checking out his butt. "You see something you like" Bryan teased. Gianna's face turned red almost immediately. She knew he was teasing but still she felt embarrassed for getting caught looking. This is her best friend after all. This wasn't like her to openly ogle Bryan. She must still be feeling horny from earlier.

Bryan took the opportunity to get a good look at Gianna. "Damn! You look good," Bryan replied shocking himself. It's not like he hadn't noticed how beautiful she was before but something was different.

"Thanks! You know Charlene is a model so I had to step up my "A" game. I threw on a little something something. It's not too much is it?" Gianna couldn't help but notice the strange look in his light brown eyes. She was starting to worry that maybe she should have went with the dress.

Bryan gulped down his wine before answering. He wasn't sure what was happening but it seemed to be getting hot in the room. "Uh no your outfits perfect. And for the record Charlene won't have anything on you tonight."

They locked gazes. Gianna moved closer and leaned in to help him smooth out his collar. She touched his strong broad chest lingering a bit. She reached around his broad shoulders to fix the back of his collar. She was leaning into him and the tips of her breasts were rubbing against the buttons on his chest. She leaned back only inches from his face. She looked up at him and then at his lips. Gianna lingered a little bit too long and as if coming out of a daze she stepped back and out of his space. She couldn't believe how much she wanted to kiss him. "What are you doing? This is Bryan, cut it out," Gianna thought to herself.

"You always did clean up well. How are we single? I just don't understand it," Gianna said as she finished her once over of Bryan trying to play off that moment.

Bryan stood there holding his breath. He for the third time today was having inappropriate thoughts about his best friend. He wasn't sure what just happened but if Gianna hadn't moved back he was going to kiss her out of her clothes and take her right on the table. "Yeah from the way you were just checking me out, I would say I clean up well too." Gianna turned red. "And please stop playing, you know you are single by choice. You let a lot of good brothers go with the lamest excuses. I on the other hand keep attracting needy women."

Gianna pulled herself together. "Well maybe you'll finally give Charlene a chance. You know she had a big crush on you back in college," Gianna said. Gianna picked up her wine glass and took a big drink from it. She put down her glass and smoothed her own shirt. That wasn't true of course but the two did flirt like it was. Charlene only had eyes for Michael but she and Bryan sharpened their skills on one another.

"You know Charlene and I are just friends. But I'm not sure if Miles or Charlene can handle us tonight. We are fine as hell. I know Miles won't be able to focus though, you may kill him in that outfit." Bryan poured another glass of wine and topped off Gianna's. Bryan reached in and removed a piece of lint from Gianna's hair. He could feel Gianna lean into his hand.

When she could breathe again she picked up the natural conversation. "Now I know why I keep you around. You're good for my ego. Poor Charlene she couldn't keep her eyes off of you during our trip to Lake Tigan. Maybe you should change and save a life." Bryan and Gianna laughed.

Charlene arrived at 6 pm sharp and rang the doorbell. She was excited to see Bryan and Gianna and more so to see this potential Michael Yvann cologne ad model.

Charlene stood at 5'11 without heels and had the clearest deep brown complexion. She was seriously considered for every anti acne campaign there was but she turned them down. She wanted it to be known that her clear skin had nothing to do with anyone's product. In other words her skins reputation wasn't for sale.

Charlene was 29 and still modeling but decided that she would start her own modeling agency. She has been in business for over 4 years now and her company had a diverse group under its belt. Right now she is looking for a new model because Charlene's ex Michael Yvann was being difficult. He normally uses her current agency's models but his recent tantrum is causing her to find someone new. His exact words "Honey, I don't see anything new and up and coming from your agency. When is your next talent search? I want to use your agency but there are so many out there."

Charlene couldn't understand it. Michael had already picked a model from her agency and he was flown to the shoot. Michael personally picked him but once he was there Michael had a fit. Charlene is sure it had everything to do with Michael not being in her pants any longer.

Hearing the doorbell, Bryan and Gianna walked toward the front door. Gianna, with her drink in one hand, opened the door with the other. Talking to Charlene over the phone for a month didn't do justice to this moment. Almost in unison Gianna and Charlene both screamed and jumped up and down. Bryan had to move fast to get Gianna's glass of wine from her and was just in time. When all the screaming and jumping stopped Bryan got a good look at Charlene.

"Hey, look at you! You haven't changed at all," Bryan said giving Charlene a hug. "Still killing the modeling game, I see. Bryan twirled her around and got a good look at her from behind.

"Yeah, I'm only taking a few dates here and there now but in my business I have to stay on point. How long has it been Bryan, a year? You still look sexy as hell. You sure you don't want to model for me. I already have the perfect client lined up." "Yeah me." Charlene thought to herself. "Ooh he is still fine. I wonder if he and Gianna are still blind to how they feel for each other."

"Oh yeah whose the client? I may be interested. I recently gotten a lot of compliments and people have been checking me out." Bryan winked at Gianna as she almost choked on her wine.

Gianna recovered and grabbed Charlene's hand ushering her into the dining room. "Anyway girl come on in, we have to catch up." Bryan followed behind laughing to himself.

Chapter 4

They all sat around the table laughing and catching up. Gianna filled her in on her latest blog idea and on how her business was going slow. Gianna just couldn't hone in on which part of her college degrees she wanted to use. Bryan started introducing his idea for Miles to be the Michael Yvann Cologne ad model.

Charlene listened hoping that Miles was the answer to her problem with Michael. Charlene knew all she really had to do was give in to Michael and accept his marriage proposal. She just couldn't be with him unless he was all in. Michael had a wondering eye at times and she couldn't be sure that he wasn't cheating while he was away on business.

Miles pulled up to the house and parked. He put his game face on and stepped out of his Audi Silver R8 Spider. He was told that the dress was casual so he wore a pair of black jeans with a button down gray striped shirt. He wore a tie earlier but opted not to wear it tonight. He was hoping to pull off a more casual modeled look. To give Charlene a preview of his assets he unbuttoned the top two buttons of his shirt. Miles looked himself over and reached for the bottle of wine and box of chocolates, walked toward the house and rang the doorbell. "A gentleman trying to impress the ladies never shows up empty handed," Miles thought to himself. "Despite what Bryan said."

Miles admired the house as he approached it. It was brick with light grey trim and dark grey shutters. The front yard was well maintained and in the driveway Miles recognized Bryan's Lincoln Navigator parked next to a Volkswagen Eos Komfort Convertible in black. Miles assumed that was Charlene's car. "Gianna must have parked in the garage. She's probably sporting a Mercedes Benz or something. Bryan said she was classy and stylish, but never one to be flashy. Either way my work is going to be cut out for me. Two confident ladies who have their own will always keep things interesting. Miles laughed out loud. I can handle it, I'm never scared. Miles laughed again thing his reference to an old rap song was perfect for the moment. Miles managed to rang the doorbell and juggle his presents in one hand.

Bryan excused himself and made his way to the door. He opened it and gave Miles a pound bringing him in for a hug. "What's up man? You ready to meet the ladies," Bryan asked. Bryan noticed the gifts and smiled, "My man now I know your right for this gig. Your mama raised you right. I had you covered though just in case you turned out to be a caveman.

"Yeah man let me at 'em. The question should be is Charlene ready for me? Man you know I wasn't about to show up empty handed and have those ladies thinking I'd forgotten my manners. I could never risk my mama finding out." They both laughed as Bryan led Miles through the house to the dining room.

He spotted Charlene right away. He'd seen enough of her campaign ads and runway shows to know exactly what she looked like. She was beautiful. She wore a gold and white striped bodice sundress with a pair of gold strappy heels. She wore her light brown hair in loose barrel curls that framed her face falling to the tips of her breasts. Breasts that were sitting right in her tight bodice sundress.

Miles found it hard to take his eyes off of Charlene. He waited while Bryan introduced him and he shook her hand and brought her in for a hug. She smelled of lavender and vanilla and she lined up perfectly against him. His arms molded perfectly around her waist. "It's a pleasure meeting you," Miles said. "Hmm you are charming aren't you," Charlene replied. Miles released his hold on her and stepped back to be introduced to the hostess. He used this as an opportunity to reel himself in. A Hurricane like Charlene can be devastating if you're not too careful.

Miles knew a little about Gianna from Bryan. The way he spoke of her was as if she was something special. Bryan was always a relationship guy which is why he wasted so much time with Tracy. Miles didn't like Tracy for Bryan. Bryan would call Miles and she would be in the back ground fussing about this or that.

She seemed very hard to please. To be fair Tracy had her hands full with Bryan. He was a work-a-holic and could lose his own head buried in work. Miles understood it was her way of trying remind him she was there, but still. A man needs to work and needs an understanding partner.

Miles reached a hand out to Gianna and pulled her in for a hug and she kissed his cheek. "You must be Gianna. Bryan's best friend. Bryan talks about you all the time so I know we will get along fine. I feel like I already know you." Gianna blushed and looked over at Bryan. "Good things of course," Miles said noticing the exchange.

"Oh! Gianna looked past Miles to Bryan. "Bryan has definitely told me a lot about you. You two used to get into so much trouble together. I'm curious, why did you and Bryan get caught in an all-girls dorm after hours? I have been dying to hear that story". Gianna linked her arm through Miles' and led him to his place at the dining room table. Everyone took their places at the table. Miles grinned and said "I'll tell you my story if you tell me about the time Bryan caught you and old what's-his-name behind the church." Gianna's blush grew a crimson red and a sly smile crossed her face. "Whatever he told you remember there are two sides to a story. Everyone laughed. "Can I get you something to drink, or are you ready to eat?" Gianna went into hostess mode. She and Bryan made plates and poured wine until everyone had eaten. Miles and Charlene were discussing business, Bryan adding his advice here and there. Gianna happy to be able to help with marketing and business advice she threw in for free. Dinner was delicious and the wine was hitting the spot.

Chapter 5

With business done, Gianna went to get the Peach Cobbler and Sweet Potato Pie. She paired it with vanilla bean ice cream. They sat around the table and enjoyed dessert. Bryan and Miles filled the ladies in on their college mischievousness. Charlene joined in with a story of her own. Bryan and Gianna were telling the story of their skinny dipping episode at Lake Tigan.

"What? I wondered why you guys were wet. I mean everything was wet. Kevin and Tracy were pissed, but you two didn't seem to notice. Laughing and carrying on I thought Kevin and Bryan were going to fight at one point," Charlene said.

"Wait, why would you say that? Kevin was glued to me the whole time after that. I couldn't seem to shake him to use the bathroom, "Gianna laughed.

Bryan glared at Charlene hoping she wouldn't continue the story. No such luck. Charlene didn't seem to understand the warning stares.

"Oh girl I thought you knew. Yeah, Kevin came looking for Bryan. We were in the living room, Mike and I, Devon and Shelly, Sarah and Sean, and Bryan and Tracy. Tracy had gone to the bathroom but she came back and heard the tail end of it. I'm sure of it."

Bryan stood up and started clearing the table. Almost everyone was focused on Charlene. Gianna noticed Bryan's face as he cleared the table but she wanted to hear the rest of the story. Bryan had left the room and headed toward the kitchen. "Hey I'm going to get the wine so we can the evening games started," Bryan said as he left.

Charlene continued. "Kevin came barreling in. He was seething mad. He walked up to Bryan and laid into him. He accused Bryan of making up some game just to see his girl. Now it all makes since, of course, but at the time we were all clueless. Truthfully, we thought Kevin had finally lost it. It became a lot clearer though. Anyway, Bryan stood up and looked at Kevin. Kevin started in again."

You think I don't know what you're doing. You think I don't see it. Maybe you're fooling yourself and Gianna is blind to it but I see. You should back off. I got this. Why don't you at least pretend a little better? You are here with Tracy right.

"What are you talking about man? Making up games is kind of what I do, ask about me. Oh, and if anyone wanted to see anyone it was clear that you were breaking your neck to see Tracy.

"Don't be ridiculous, I was only looking out for her because you were busy drooling after Gianna. Someone had to make sure your girl didn't fall and break her neck." Kevin fumed back at Bryan.

"Look man, for the record. I'm here with Tracy, I've been here and I'm not going nowhere. Bryan started to walk away but he stopped and turned and said, "If you got it, why you out here talking to me. We are all grown and we don't have to do a damn thing we don't want to. If you didn't want to play you know what you had to do.

"You know what you're doing. You're trying to cause a problem for me with Gianna. I know you tell her she can do better than me. Who are you talk? Kevin was now in Bryan's face. Devon stepped in to put some space between them to calm the situation down.

"Oh, I'm cool Devon". Bryan assured Devon that he was in control seeing him back up Kevin. He looked back at Kevin, "I don't have to do or say anything you will mess this up all on your own. And yeah I am here with Tracy why don't you remember that. I see how you look at her. I see those wheels turning. Just waiting for your opening, huh? Just like with Keisha. Yeah she told me about it." Bryan started moving toward Kevin. "Gianna is my best friend, man, and if you do anything to hurt her again, I will hurt you."

Bryan stood staring at Kevin. Kevin looked like he was going to say more but he noticed Tracy in the doorway. Kevin turned around but said "just be happy in the friend zone she put you in and we won't have no problems." He left the room.

"It was Mike's turn to be peace keeper stepping into Bryan's path. Bryan looked like he was going to really hurt Kevin." Done her story Charlene sipped her wine. She noticed that Bryan had left. Gianna seemed shocked "You really didn't know that happened?" Charlene asked Gianna.

"NO. Kevin and I were supposed to leave that night so we did. Neither one ever led on. Anyway they seemed to have buried the hatchet since then because we spent so much time together, the four of us, since that happened." Gianna pasted a smile on her face. She excused herself and went into the kitchen to find Bryan.

Gianna knew she'd only partially told the truth. They did spend a lot of time together after that but it wasn't the same. Kevin and Bryan's relationship was strained and if she was honest Tracy grew distant. She noticed the glares the guys gave each other but assumed that there was some inside testosterone joke she didn't understand. Gianna recalled a conversation between her and Tracy.

They were out shopping for a birthday present for Bryan. Tracy had decided to buy him a leather ledger for his new business he'd started. Gianna thought it was a cool gift but it wasn't personal it was more of a friend gift. Tracy and Bryan had been dating for at least a year and a half, and it was definitely enough time to get personal. Gianna made a suggestion that Tracy should have a lingerie photo taken, personalize it and have it framed. She went on to tell her that she and Bryan had talked about things they wanted and how Bryan had mentioned that some years ago. She thought Bryan would have forgotten the conversation by now and it would truly be a good surprise for him that he'd like. Gianna thought Tracy would come out looking like the perfect girlfriend who knew just what Bryan would like. Tracy, didn't seem to share in the sentiments. She bought the ledger anyway and made up an excuse cut short their shopping trip. Hell Gianna didn't even get help with her gift for Bryan.

Later that day, all four of them were at Bryan's house and they were just about to exchange gifts. Kevin offered up a lame key chain that came stock with his new car. Bryan was unbothered. Then Tracy excited she rushed to go next. Bryan was happy about his ledger and kissed her. Gianna pulled her present from behind her back. Bryan opened it and laughed then fell over laughing. Gianna had kept the idea she'd shared with Tracy. She replaced the lingerie photo with a picture of her and Bryan when they were in college.

It was the first time she got drunk and Bryan had been equally drunk. Charlene snuck up on them and took the picture just as Gianna was reaching behind Bryan for her red cup, and Bryan was leaning forward for something off camera. The angle in which Charlene took the picture made Bryan and Gianna look like they were kissing. It didn't help that the moment the picture was taken both of their eyes were closed. It was a running joke between their college crew. Gianna thought it was funny so when he had the same reaction they both laughed for about 5 minutes with tears and everything.

Tracy finally having had enough jumped up and rushed to the closet for her coat. She said her goodbyes and left with an excuse of an early day the next day. Kevin was right on her heels only he didn't bother to say a word, He just left. After reading the situation, really looking at the picture and the caption she understood better. It only took her years to see it. Bryan and Tracy split up shortly after that and Kevin and Gianna's problems began around that time. They broke up and made up too many times to count before ending things. Bryan only said of his break up that Tracy was too needy and was always nagging him. Gianna now wonders if Tracy was nagging him about her. In Gianna's mind she and Kevin's break up had nothing to do with Bryan or that night but everything to do with Keisha and Tiffany, and oh who can name them all. But now looking back she knew it had a lot to do with that night for Kevin.

Gianna hurried to the kitchen to find Bryan. Bryan was hot. He couldn't believe Charlene was rehashing this argument between him and Kevin. He thought he swore everyone to secrecy. Suddenly he remembered Charlene and Mike left a little after Gianna and that punk ass Kevin did, so he missed talking to them. Bryan wanted to hurt Kevin that day, but he knew he would have to explain it to Gianna. He worked too hard to suppress his feelings in order to be 100 % her best friend and nothing more. He couldn't risk her knowing that he has loved her since the day she gave him his first kiss.

Bryan moved to the bucket of ice housing the wine. He removed it and began to open it. The Pop of the cork startled him out of his daze, causing him to realize he wasn't alone. He put a smile on his face and sat the wine bottle down. Turning to face the visitor he wasn't surprised to see Gianna standing in the doorway.

Chapter 6

Charlene took another sip of her wine and looked to the bottle for a refill. As if reading her mind, Miles was on top of it moving to pour her another glass.

"So, how long have you known Bryan," Charlene asked. She wanted to know if Miles knew how Bryan felt about Gianna. Charlene was thinking of bringing Miles up to speed on her developing plan to get Bryan and Gianna to finally give each other the time of day. She was hoping Bryan's idea for a drinking game would help them loosen up.

Once she got them to see things her way she would worry about her own fun. Charlene wanted to find out if Miles could mix business with a little pleasure and not get attached. Already deciding that if this night turned cozy Miles would definitely get lucky. She was single enough, for now, and as far as she knew so was Miles.

Formulating a plan in her mind to have a little fun while playing love connection. She drank her wine and listened to Miles recount a story about a time when they played a Bryan Stillwater drinking game. Miles' story was animated and he was funny and charming. As Miles continued the story Charlene had her answer. Miles would be perfect to cross that line with and not have the need for a restraining order afterwards.

Miles looked at Charlene as he told her about Bryan's drinking game. He wasn't sure if he should tell her the details but he was all in and the details were the best parts. Bryan's drinking games were the best and always ended in everyone sleeping over. This night Bryan was in rare form. By the end of the night everyone had paired off and cozied up for the night. Bryan woke up with Big Booty Belinda Strong. "This was a big deal" he explained to Charlene, "because Bryan is a relationship guy."

Miles told Charlene that he woke up the next morning with sexy ass Vanessa Starks. Charlene laughed and seemed to enjoy the story. Miles was glad for that because he was hoping this drinking game would end with him and Charlene finding their own cozy location in the house. "Damn she if fine," Miles told himself.

Miles continued to look across the table at Charlene noting how extremely attractive she was. "Man a brother really had to play this one cool to have a chance in hell with a girl like Charlene," Miles thought to himself. "Yeah "a" brother, but Charlene wouldn't be able to resist this brother." Charlene was definitely a good catch. She handled her business, and held her own in a conversation. Miles was looking forward to getting to know her a lot better.

"Do you think they are ok in there," Miles asked trying not to completely wake up the dragon. Mike adjusted himself in his seat. Charlene was thankful for the Segway to her plan.

"Yeah, they have a good handle on each other. If anyone can calm Bryan down it would be Gianna. They just need a few minutes, that's all. Hopefully they are confessing their true feelings so we can finally get rid of Kevin and Tracy." Charlene made the mistake of looking Miles right in the eyes. "I do hope we don't have to start our own drinking game without them."

Miles smiled slyly. "Sounds like you are ready to advance this night, huh? Why don't we move this party to the family room? They will find us when they are through." Miles was beginning to think that undoing the two buttons was a brilliant idea. He noticed Charlene's bedroom eyes but thought it was just him. Now she wants to start the party without all the guests, which could only be good news for him.

"Smart and handsome, hmm. Don't forget the wine." Charlene followed Miles into the Livingroom.

Charlene and Miles moved the party to the family room. They sat down on the couch and began talking. Charlene found herself excited for this evening's games. She always loved Bryan's made up games. She started telling Miles about when Bryan found Tracy's "SEX Escapades, The Game" and decided to make it a drinking game. The rules were if you didn't do what the card said you had to take a shot. "Well we played the game, and let's just say we learned a lot about each other that night. I am hoping this night will be just as interesting." They both locked eyes and smiled.

Charlene reached for her glass and once again on cue Miles was there to refill it. They'd had a few glasses already so Charlene didn't have the steadiest of hands. Miles held her hand steadying the glass and poured the wine. After pouring it he took it and sat it on the table while moving in closer. He leaned in and Charlene moved forward. His lips meeting hers she moaned shocking herself. His hand made its way to the small of her back as he deepened the kiss. They finally came up for air and laughed nervously. They started up a conversation about the evenings drinking games to cool down the heat.

Bryan and Gianna returned from the kitchen laughing. They found Miles and Charlene in the family room engrossed in conversation. Gianna was worried that leaving them for so long would cause them to get bored and end the evening early. She should have known that Charlene would keep the party going.

Bryan was holding the bottles of Paul Masson Peach and Amsterdam Pineapple, ready to move the evening along. Gianna had snacks and shot glasses. She brought Chips and dip out for the light weights. Miles stood to help Gianna carry the shot glasses and Charlene helped arrange the snacks. Bryan sat down and opened the Paul Masson Peach first. Gianna sat down and started to apologize for leaving Miles and Charlene to entertain themselves for so long.

Bryan filled the shot glasses and asked everyone how they were feeling. "Are you ready to spend the night, or do any of you have to wake up early tomorrow?"

"Man, I know you so I came prepared," Miles said. Miles was forewarned about how this evening may end. He also knew that if Bryan was in charge of the entertainment he would need an overnight bag and his own special brew in the morning. He looked at Charlene, "I am ready to get this evening started.

"Just so you know I have plenty of room and you're all more than welcome to stay," Gianna added. "Miles I didn't know how far back you and Bryan went, but now I'm sure you know there is no use trying to leave tonight. Miles smiled, "Thanks Gianna Bryan was right about you." "Well he just tells all my business, huh." Everyone laughed.

It was Charlene's turn to decide. She was busy setting up the table. She had a thing for everything having a place. Feeling like all eyes was on her she looked up and found all eyes were on her. "Oh, you don't even have to ask, I'm down for whatever. My overnight bag is in the car." Everyone laughed.

"I guess my reputation precedes itself," Bryan said laughing. Bryan started the night off with a mild game. He wanted to test the waters and keep everyone comfortable. He hoped that Charlene didn't ruin the evening by mentioning punk ass Kevin. Bryan knew she was cool so he wasn't going to let that ruin the rest of the evening. Gianna missed that whole encounter, mainly because he protected her from it. Bryan shook it off and was determined to enjoy the evening. "Well I think we can begin harmless enough with a little Truth or Dare shots.

To show good faith Bryan went first and he chose dare. He had to take a shot before doing whatever the group came up with. He was dared to finish the next three rounds in only his boxers and socks. The kicker was that he had to give them a strip tease while taking off the clothes. This was Charlene's big bright idea of course Bryan thought. He stood up and after taking another shot he started his strip tease.

Charlene and Gianna fanned themselves as Bryan began taking off his pants. By the time he revealed his wash board abs both ladies reached for a shot. "Charlene remember, you are next. Bryan threw his shirt at her. Charlene stood up and motioned for him to bring it on. "I can handle anything you throw at me Bryan. I am not scared." Everyone laughed.

Gianna was unbelievably hot and she couldn't seem to cool off. At one point she had to excuse herself from the room to bring out some ice. Of course Miles called foul. He felt that ice would water down the shots. Eventually the ladies convinced the fellas to allow it. Gianna had no intentions of using the ice but needed a few minutes to collect herself.

Gianna returned to the room but her seat was directly across from Bryan. She found her eyes drawn to him and his muscular frame. She couldn't even think straight. She used the chips and dip to distract herself from openly ogling his sensual frame. "Really Gianna get it together. It's Bryan," Gianna admonished herself. You have played this game a million times what is wrong with you?"

Charlene nudged Gianna as if she read her mind and knew she needed to be saved. It was Charlene's turn and Miles wanted to do the honors. He asked "truth, dare or consequences."

"Hmm, I'm feeling very daring tonight. I choose dare. Charlene took her shot and waited for her challenge.

Miles smiled a devilish smile. "Charlene I dare you to make out with Gianna right here right now.

Gianna wasn't shocked. Bryan's games can get very personal. She looked at Charlene and waited for her to make her move. Charlene turned around to face Gianna. Gianna sat back against the back of the couch. Charlene leaned in close and kissed Gianna's lips softly.

Gianna thought it would blow the boys minds if they took the kiss to another level. She reached up and grabbed Charlene's breasts and deepened the kiss. Charlene followed her lead and began to caress Gianna's breasts and allowed her tongue to dance with Gianna's. They moaned and felt each other up. Charlene leaned over

Gianna and was nearly on top of her, when they heard someone clear their throat.

Miles was in heaven. He never thought that Charlene would accept the dare. He was prepared for her to drink hot sauce as her consequence. His mind was blown. Bryan the one who cleared his throat wasn't shocked. These two have done this before. They are quite the professionals at it because of Bryan's famous drinking games. It never gets old though. Bryan had to adjust himself so he wouldn't reveal just how much he enjoyed it.

Miles was the first to speak. "Man why did you break that up. It was just getting good.

"Yeah but you're not the one in your boxers," Bryan laughed.

"Well boys put your tongues back in your mouths," Gianna and Charlene said in unison.

Everyone laughed. The evening progressed. Bryan earned his clothes back. There were no more make out sessions. Bryan decided that this was the last round. He had another game idea. By this time with one bottle of Paul Masson gone everyone was feeling loose and very comfortable with each other.

It was Gianna's turn, she took her shot and waited. "Truth, dare or consequences," 'Bryan asked her. Gianna chose dare. I dare you to pick one of us and simulate your favorite position during sex."

Chapter 7

The sexual tension in the room was so thick you could cut it with a butter knife. Gianna looked Bryan directly in his eyes and took her shot. She stood slowly and seductively walked over to Bryan. She leaned over him revealing her breasts through the neckline of the shirt. She hovered just close enough to kiss him. "I am going to make him beg me to stop," Gianna thought.

Bryan was trying to play it cool. He sat with his arms spread out across the back of the couch. "This women is playing with fire. She's not even playing fair." Bryan was doing everything he could, thinking of baseball, work, anything. None of it was taking his mind off of the smoking hot women in front of him.

Gianna kicked up the fire a notch and seductively climbed into his lap. She placed both knees at either side of Bryan and sat down onto his lap. Even through his pants she could tell she was winning. She began to grind on him as she held him by his shoulders. She felt him grow thick and long and she was enjoying gyrating on every inch of it. Everything and everyone but Bryan faded away.

Thinking about baseball and work wasn't cutting it. Bryan began to unravel. He put both hands on Gianna's ample ass and squeezed. He could feel his cock's fullness with every move Gianna made. He grabbed her by the waist and increased the pressure from her on to his dick. He could feel her pussy lips through her leggings. He stood up. She bounced up and down on him as he squeezed her ass pressing her pussy against his hard package.

Miles looked across at Charlene. Charlene was enjoying the show and at some point she started rubbing on her breasts and one hand disappeared between her legs. Miles moved to sit next to her. He was hard as a rock just from the show alone but grew even harder watching Charlene caress her breasts and rub on her pussy. He moved to replace her hand on her breasts with his. He thought that was a good way to let her know he was there. She turned to him and pulled him toward her to kiss him. He kissed her back and started rubbing tiny circles on her nipples. She climbed into his lap and deepened the kiss.

Everyone was feeling the alcohol and had slipped into a lust filled trance. Gianna started kissing Bryan's neck, and jawline, as she made her way to his lips.

His lips were soft, thick and juicy. She'd never kissed him like this before. She felt bold and free with Bryan. She felt his hard dick through her leggings and she just couldn't get close enough.

Bryan was lost. He found himself walking toward the stairs, up the stairs and managed to kick open her bedroom door. He carried her to the bed. Just looking at the bed brought back his memory of Gianna pleasuring herself. He groaned and quickly laid her down on her back and immediately covered her with is body. She continued to kiss and mesmerize him with her tongue. She sucked on his ear lobe and teased him with her teeth. He was grinding himself against her and feeling on her breasts. He began to move down her body touching every inch. He pulled up her shirt and she sat up for him to remove her bra. He cupped her ample breasts and began to lick and suck and tease them with his tongue.

Gianna groaned as she wrapped her legs around Bryan and continued to grind against him. She reached for his shirt and slowly pulled it above his head. Bryan obliged and threw the shirt to the floor. Gianna took the time to admire his chest and abs rubbing her hands along the ridged muscles. Memorizing every inch as she made her way up to his handsome face. She never noticed Bryan this way and she felt like an idiot for not seeing it before now. He was fine and his body matched perfectly against hers. Everything he did felt right, from his touch to his mouth, to his tongue.

Bryan looked down at Gianna and took it all in. She was incredibly sexy in every way. She released him from her leg grip and he noticed her wiggling out of her leggings. He let out a groan as his dick did jumping jacks in his boxers. He was now very uncomfortable in his boxers. Once Gianna's leggings and panties were off Bryan went into overdrive. He tenderly kissed her from her forehead to her toes. He made his way back and stopped at her valley. He licked her inner thighs, then licked her clit. He tongued her opening revealing her nectar and back to her thighs. He teased her like this and had Gianna gyrating and pleading for more.

Gianna wanted to rip off the rest of Bryan's clothes and jump on him. She never wanted anyone to make love to her so bad. He just wasn't close enough she wanted him inside of her now. She begged and pleaded for more but Bryan kept teasing her and bringing her closer to the edge then he'd lick her inner thigh. Bryan began sucking on her clit and then he put his finger in her. A wave of pleasure took over Gianna and she came immediately.

Bryan couldn't wait any longer, he was more than ready. He pulled off his clothes, slid on a condom and entered Gianna in one motion. She gasped and he groaned. Gianna was so tight, warm and wet he nearly finished before he started. Bryan stayed still in her warm folds allowing her to adjust to his size and girth. He almost came just sliding his dick in her sweet pussy so he took this time to regain control. She couldn't wait she tried to move him in deeper with her legs.

Bryan moved in closer his dick pulsing in her as she felt so good. Gianna moved and gyrated underneath him. He relished her every movement and locked eyes with her. He leaned down and kissed her softly and began to move in and out slowly at first.

Gianna felt every inch of him, loved it and never wanted him to stop. Bryan started off slow and then his rhythm picked up and she was once again close to the edge. She tilted her ass of the bed allowing Bryan to go deeper. He pumped in and out taking her further and further to heaven. He began to pulsate and she began to vibrate all around his dick. He let out a groan and Gianna moaned as they climaxed together.

Bryan rolled over moving Gianna on top of him. He slid out so she removed the condom and put it in the trash next to the bed. She laid there in heaven, on top of him. He wrapped her up in his arms. She sat up and began kissing his neck and jawline. That was all it took. Bryan was hard as a rock. He lifted Gianna up and slid himself right back into heaven. They continued that way for hours until they both fell asleep together.

Gianna woke up first. She kept hearing knocking on the wall. She sat up on Bryan and realized that is was coming from the room next door. "Miles and Charlene are getting it in. Umm listen to her he is doing the damn thing," Gianna said. Bryan opened his eyes and looked up at Beautiful caramel breast in his face. He reached out and cupped them. Gianna looked down into his light brown eyes and gave into her body's needs. She playfully rubbed her C cups in his face.

Bryan's touch and the sound of sex from the other room drove Gianna crazy. She reached down, finding Bryan hard she positioned herself above him and eased him in. She rode him like her life depended on it. He moaned and made sucking sounds as he enjoyed the delicious caramel breasts in his face. He gave each one a fair amount of time. Never one to be out done, He flipped Gianna over and took her from behind with her ass in the air. Gianna moaned and groaned into her pillow. Her pussy never felt this good.

Bryan slowed his pace, easing out to the tip then slowly putting his complete length into her. He did this over and over as Gianna's body rose to meet him. She came three times before he finally succumbed to his own orgasm.

Chapter 8

Emerging after what felt like a lifetime, Gianna and Miles sat at the kitchen table. Miles and Charlene had left quietly leaving them alone. They moved seamlessly around the kitchen making breakfast and cleaning up last night's evidence.

Gianna was a million miles away. She couldn't believe how many times she orgasmed, screamed out his name, and begged for more as if he was the last drop of water. Also on her mind was "what now?" She wasn't sure. Bryan has always been there but as her best friend, she didn't want to lose that ever. "Maybe Bryan feels the same way, I mean really, how is this supposed to work now?" The words were out of her mouth before she could stop them. "Um what happens now," Gianna asked Bryan.

Bryan was in a haze. He was so elated, he couldn't explain it. Last night was the best sex everything he'd ever experienced in his life. This couldn't have happened at a better time. Now we can explore and see how we can make this friendship more of the relationship it should be. "I guess we see where this will lead. I think a connection this strong shouldn't be ignored." Bryan reached over to take Gianna's hand.

Gianna grew more and more scared. "What if this hurts our friendship? Aren't you surprised by this? Was it the alcohol? That has to explain our behavior. We have never even kissed, let alone made love." Gianna moved away from the table and walked over to the window. "I mean how did you do all of those things to me? I lost count of how many orgasms, and boy that tongue is a lethal weapon. But I don't know. It was like you knew me better that I knew myself."

Bryan followed and wrapped his arms around her. They stood there for what seemed like hours. "Gianna I think we owe it to ourselves to see where this goes. I never knew making love could be so, so good. We connected, we were in sync, and we fit. Everyone sees it but us, and now I see it. I see you." Alright Bryan now bring it on home, tell her how you feel, Bryan thought to himself.

Gianna turned around to face Bryan and looked directly into his eyes. "Bryan I ....", "Gianna I....", they both said in unison. The doorbell rang startling both of them. Gianna left Bryan's warm embrace reluctantly and headed toward the door. The bell rang again. "Ugh I really hope this is important" Gianna thought. "I mean we need to finish this. It's a lot to take in." Gianna opened the door.

"Hello, can I come in?

Kevin Reynolds was standing on Gianna's doorstep. His hands interlocked at the front of his pants. He was clean shaven and had on a fresh crisp suit. He wanted to talk. Bryan was still in the kitchen and he wanted to discuss "us" and "more". Gianna felt trapped. She couldn't breathe. "How did things get to be so complicated? My past and present colliding was not how a Sunday morning should start."

She never thought she would see Kevin again and didn't think she would be inviting him in. "Kevin I am entertaining company, you have three minutes. What do you want?" Gianna folded her arms to wait for his response. She was a little relieved to have a second to think about Bryan.

Bryan watched from the dining room. Gianna looked like she'd seen a ghost. Something else happened, she looked relieved. Gianna looked almost happy to see Kevin. The guy who broke her heart over and over again. Unable to look on any longer, Bryan gathered his things. He dressed and left out the back door. He made his way to his car and took one last look at the house. Kevin was no longer on the front step she invited him inside.

Gianna waited nervously she knew how Bryan felt about Kevin. She didn't want a repeat of their last encounter. Spending the night trying to convince officer Reaves not to arrest them was hard. Neither men seemed to understand the gravity of the situation and continued to go after one another. Kevin had been caught red handed by Bryan. Bryan went to the Diamond Club for a bachelor party and spotted Kevin hugged up with Yvette, the ex. Bryan introduced himself and watched Kevin turn white, while Yvette acted like she was the main chick again. She was oblivious or didn't care about the fact that Bryan was Gianna's best friend and that Gianna wasn't out of the picture. Kevin eased out of Yvette's grip and made an excuse to leave. He left Yvette there and ran straight to Gianna's house only Bryan beat him there. When Kevin tried to lie Bryan punched him in his eye. He still has a little scar on his eye lid from it. Gianna smiled to herself. "Bryan has always been there, even then," she thought.

"I was hoping maybe to talk to you about something." Kevin walked past her and into the dining room. She moved to block his access to the living room just in time. He took the hint and pulled out a chair and sat down.

"What is it you want to talk about that wouldn't warrant a call first? This better be good." Gianna sat across from him. "He has some nerve," Gianna thought.

Bryan started the car and began driving away from Gianna and back into the friend zone. "Well at least you finally told her how you feel, well almost." Bryan said out loud to himself. He drove for a long time. He drove past his house. Bryan didn't want to be alone. He continued driving in a daze. He drove until he was outside of Tracy's house. He sat there looking at the front door. "How did I end up here?"

Bryan recalled the time he had last seen Tracy. They ran into one another at the Mayor's birthday party. Tracy made her way over to say hello. Bryan hadn't expected to see her so he was taken aback by how beautifully she looked. She asked Bryan how he was and what he'd been up to. They fell right back into place. They were good together.

Later that night Bryan took her home. There wasn't any hesitation as to whether or not to follow her inside. They moved fluidly together. Tracy changed into a sexy low cut maxi dress that clung to all her curves. Bryan took off his suit jacket and loosened his tie. They sat and talked for hours.

"Maybe this is where I should be. " Bryan looked up at Tracy's front door. Surprised it was now open and Tracy was standing in the doorway. Tracy waved for him to come in. He sighed and cut the engine and exited the car. He left his cell phone plugged into the cigarette lighter.

Once inside, Bryan could smell the sweet scent of fresh homemade apple pie. He knew Sunday was Tracy's favorite day of the week. She told him of the special home cooked meals she grew up eating on that day after church. Everyone would gather around the table and talk about current events and their hopes and dreams. Bryan knew Tracy hoped to continue that tradition with her own family one day.

"How long were you sitting out there? I almost went and tapped on the window." Tracy turned to look at Bryan for a response.

Bryan looked at her as if seeing her for the first time. Her hair was up on top of her head in a messy bun. She had the faintest amount of make up on with deep plum lipstick on her full lips. She was dressed comfortably in an off the shoulder t-shirt that read "Natural Hair if you dare", and a pair of purple tights with pom-pom socks on. Bryan took it all in. "You know what I couldn't even tell you. I don't even remember the drive here," Bryan said. "I just drove, I needed to think. "Oh, well that's not alarming." Tracy said, "Come on."

Moving through the house toward the kitchen, Tracy and Bryan continued to catch up. Tracy was putting the finishing touches on her Sunday dinner and Bryan was helping with the dishes. They moved in a calm quiet as they finished their tasks. Bryan was just grateful for the busy work. The company wasn't so bad either. Tracy hummed her favorite gospel song and danced as she worked.

Once everything was done they sat at the table and had a slice of one of the pies and some warm milk. Tracy waited Bryan out as long as she could. "Are you going to tell me what's wrong? And don't tell me nothing I know you too well for that.

Bryan looked up at Tracy and smiled. He knew he painted her out to be a self-absorbed brat and he was wrong for that. Bryan realized he wasn't giving Tracy a fair chance. She was always there for him when he let her be. "One things for sure Tracy wouldn't sleep with me then invite her ex into the house with me still in there." Bryan couldn't let the images of Gianna's relived face and then the empty porch out of his mind. He looked up at Tracy. She was staring at him. She smiled and ate a piece of pie. "Look I won't force it out of you. I need your help with something. Follow me into the bedroom."

This is what Bryan did best he was good with his hands and solving other people's problems. He followed Tracy to her room and relieved to have something to take his mind off of things.

He remembered a time when Tracy tried to reach for something in her attic and hurt her ankle. She called Bryan and they spent the next three weeks playing every board game they could find. He even let her slide when he caught her cheating. They spent long nights by the fireplace enjoying every inch of each other. Most nights they stayed up talking all through the night. She was always easy to talk too. No surprise he ended up there.

"I guess I just needed to sort some things out is all. I really don't want to get into it." Bryan knew he couldn't mention any part of this morning to anyone, and he for damn sure couldn't mention last night to Tracy. Tracy turned and looked at Bryan. Tracy knew something was wrong now. "I didn't say anything. I'm here if you need to talk. Anyway, can you please see what you can do about...this?"

Tracy pulled down the attic ladder. She gestured for him to go up the stairs. Tracy knew what he needed, to feel important. Which meant keep him busy. She needed to get the Fourth of July decorations up before July. What better way than with help? "I need the Fourth of July stuff down. You know what happened the last time I went up, I came down on my ankle."

"Nah we don't want that. I got it." Bryan was thankful for the distraction. He went up the ladder and shifted around a few boxes until he came across the decorations. Something else caught his eye. He moved closer to some old photo albums and dusted them off. He opened them and smiled. Tracy had kept their photos and souvenirs. They were all there in the boxes.

Tracy was in the living room, on the phone. She'd cleared a path for the boxes. Now she was just waiting for

Bryan to bring them down. "Yeah he was outside my house this morning. I don't know girl. No I've seen him around. We are friends, I'm not expecting anything. He has to first admit he has feelings for Gianna, then convince me that she doesn't feel the same way. I'm tired of feeling like the third wheel in my own relationship." Tracy laughed dryly. "Then he has to take time to get over that. Which would take too long." Tracy looked around her house. She was doing just fine. "I can't see me waiting around for that. I deserve to be his first thoughts outside of God. Yeah, I know. He is a good man and we were good together, but is it enough? Do we have a future? There was a long pause where Shondra was imputing her two cents. "Yes I hear you, but I am not falling back down that rabbit hole. I'm okay dating for now. My last date with Jonathan was really good.

Tracy hadn't started dating right away. She was sure that Bryan would see that the birthday present Gianna gave him was entirely too personal. The inside jokes they share undermined their relationship. She had truly had enough of being the third wheel. She surrendered and let Gianna win. She only wanted to Bryan to be happy but not at her expense. When she did start dating it was rough. Max was a jerk, Seth was very snobby, and now Jonathan. Jonathan was okay. Tracy was waiting for the other shoe to drop there.

"He took me to the new restaurant downtown, "The Dream House. You know the one where every section has a theme and each floor has different genres of music. Well danced on every floor. He was pretty good too." Tracy stood up and mimicked the dances. She was in mid twirl when she saw Bryan leaning against the doorway smiling. "Oh crap girl let me call you back. I'm in here dancing and making a complete full of myself. Bryan just walked in. He laughed so hard.

"Boy sneaking up on me will get you hurt. She laughed. "Did you find the boxes okay? Bryan, trying to compose himself, answered with a wave of his hands. She saw the mountain of boxes and dreaded it immediately. "Ugh, why do I have to be miss sunshine all the time? Maybe this year I'll only put up a few things."

Bryan knew better that's why he brought them all down. "Yeah right. You know you're going to have all these boxes emptied before noon." He looked at his watch oblivious of the time until now. "It's 9:30 am now, if we hurry we can get it all done. Tracy looked up. "We? Uh okay, beats spending all day doing it. Come on."

After putting up all the decorations, Tracy found a box that they must have missed. She groaned. "Bryan you won't believe this but we missed a box. I didn't know I had this much stuff. Hey will you be around to help me take it all down. Tracy laughed to herself. She walked over to the box and leaned over to pick it up. "Wow, this is heavy she yelled out. I'll wait for you to lift it.

Bryan finished his shower and through on some clothes he had in the car. He looked at himself in the mirror. "What are you doing? That box can open up old wounds. What do you want here? You heard what she told Shondra, she wants to be put first. What about Gianna?" Bryan clinched his fists and banged them down on the counter. He was tired of thinking about Gianna. He wanted to be happy.

Bryan entered the living room. He saw that Tracy had brought in some milk and more pie. He lifted the box onto the couch and sat down next to Tracy. "No Bryan I think those are the decorations, we must have missed them. I think we have enough decoration up so no need to put up more." Tracy tried to stop him before he created more work. She was tired and just wanted to relax.

Bryan looked at her with his charming eyes and opened the box. "Do you remember when we first met? I was sitting at the counter at "Sweet Mamas" eating breakfast. You were just coming in. You wore your yellow striped shirt and white skirt. You had some strappy little things on your feet with your pretty pink toenail polish peeking through. Do you remember what I asked you?" Bryan's hands disappeared into the box.

Tracy's head snapped up, she nearly dropped her plate. "Bryan? What. What are you doing? Tracy was confused. She felt like this was coming out of nowhere. "This couldn't have anything to do with why he showed up at my house this morning. Could it?"

Bryan pulled out a picture frame with a picture of the two of them taken on the very day they met. Tracy dresses has Bryan had described. Bryan was dressed in a white polo shirt and a pair of jeans. He had his arm around her and they were both laughing. "Do you remember?"

"Yeah Bryan, of course I remember." Tracy laughed thinking about what Bryan said to her all those years ago. "You said, I was saving this seat for the most beautiful women in the world." Tracy smiled. "Then you got down and helped me up. You told me to order whatever I wanted and then we talked for hours." Tracy was warmed by the memory, but she sensed she was close to the rabbit hole. "I see you found the box I kept of us. Sure we can go through it. Maybe you want a few things back." Tracy inched closer to see what else was in the box.

Bryan reached for her hands, taking them in his. "Tracy, I want you back." Bryan rushed to say, "On your terms this time and at your pace." Bryan pulled her to her feet and brought her up against his body. "Can we talk, really talk, about us.

Tracy tried to pull back her hands but he held them firmly. He her up to her feet and quickly pulled her to him. She felt swept off her feet. Bryan always had that effect on her. Tracy looked up into his eyes and saw what she'd hoped for. He saw her, really saw her. There were no distractions he didn't look occupied. His attention was trained on her and he waited for her to answer. "Yes, I would entertain the conversation. If that will help you with this mid-life crisis you seem to be going through. Tracy laughed.

It was all she could do. This was new for her. She'd only really had his attention completely the first day they'd met. Now he was offering her what she wanted. "What do I want," she thought to herself.

Bryan looked down into her eyes. "I overlooked her for so long worrying about the wrong things and people. I have to do what makes me happy."

Chapter 9

Kevin spoke first, "I'm sorry for not calling first. I need to know what you have decided. Will you help me?" Kevin stood in the foyer for what seemed like forever. He had rushed over after speaking to his mother. Things didn't look good. He needed to speed up the plan.

Gianna adjusted her robe and tried to fix her hair as best she could. "Why did you let him in? Why is he even here so early? He said I had time to think about it." Gianna's mind was racing. Bryan was still here and his most hated person in the world right now is in my house. "Kevin come into the dining room. We can talk there. I have company so let me tend to them and get dressed. Do me a favor stay here, I will bring us some coffee."

Kevin heard company and perked up. Somewhat excited to be breaking up her little date, he couldn't help but smirk. He sat down at the table. "She has to go along with my plan. I'll only tell her what she needs to know. My Dad won't get away with this. I'll make her fall in love with me again and then we will get married. Even if I have to exaggerate the truth little bit." Kevin thought of a millions ways to approach Gianna without alarming her. He wanted to keep it light and simple until he could get he into the car. "Getting her to into the car is half the battle won."

Kevin looked around the room. He knew it well. They'd spent numerous dinners there and plenty of argument happened there too. Kevin knew how to get out of the dog house though, he always had. Gianna had a bleeding heart, and it was her weakness. "She'll help me, I just have to make sure good ole' Dad played his part. Kevin took a seat at the head of the table. He smiled pleased that the beginning stages of his plan was finally coming together.

Gianna searched the entire house but Bryan had gone. She quickly showered and dressed. She made a mental note to call Bryan as soon as she got rid of Kevin. She couldn't help it but a sinking feeling was telling her that Bryan saw Kevin. "No, if Bryan had seen Kevin he would have tried to kick his ass, not leave." Gianna rushed to the kitchen, straightening up as she moved through the house. She mustered up some coffee and a couple of muffins.

Kevin stood as she entered the room. He noticed that Gianna thought this was a social call. He had to be quick. "Gianna we really don't have a lot of time. I got the call from my mom this morning. Angela and Martin will be here this afternoon. Donald and Renee will be here this evening. We should be there before they arrive. Uncle Ralph, Diane and the kids will be here tomorrow. Angela and Donald will stay at the house and I thought we should too." Kevin kept talking. He knew that if he left an opening Gianna would catch her breath and he would have to beg. It was much better to overload her with information to build the momentum and then get her body moving. Kevin started walking toward her and ushering her out toward the hallway. "We really need to get you some clothes packed and gather up all the things you'll need for a few weeks."

Gianna was flustered she found herself moving and trying to listen at the same time. She had questions and she needed them answered. Gianna dug her heels in and stopped all motion. She whirled around and put up her hands. "Wait a minute. What are you talking about? I spoke to you two weeks ago. You told me that I had time to decide what I wanted to do. I am not leaving my house to live for however long at your parents' house. I am not in this that deep. Now start explaining. What you are talking about?"

Kevin expected this but he'd hoped he could at least have gotten her in the car first. "Gianna you know my father's condition. He has stage four cancer and he isn't doing well. I don't have time for this. Grab somethings and I will go into greater detail on the way." Kevin moved her along. He pulled the suitcases from the hall closet and lugged them into the bedroom.

Gianna was wrapped up in Kevin's movement. She watched him remove things from her closet and pack them away. She watched as her designer dresses and slacks went into the suitcases instead of a garment bag. She cringed. "Move Kevin, you're wrinkling my clothes. I can't even believe I am going to help you. You have to be the biggest ass hole I've ever dated. If it wasn't for your mother I wouldn't have even taken your calls." Gianna was irritated now. She wasn't sure how Kevin wanted her help, outside of moral support, but she was sure he had an ulterior motive. She would find out soon enough.

They finished loading the luggage into the car "Kevin I forgot something and I need to set the alarm. I'll be right back." Gianna headed back into the house. She wanted to call Bryan. "Voicemail, shit. Hey Bryan it's Gianna. You left without saying goodbye. I wanted to have that talk with you but you won't believe who showed up. Anyway call me. I'm heading out of town for a few weeks so call my cell. When I get back we need, to have that talk."

Gianna didn't mention Kevin, as her reason for leaving town. She knew she would need to see him face to face to explain that she is helping Kevin. So she left him out of the message. She called Charlene next to check in with her. She left her with the same vague information just in case Charlene sees Bryan first. "I feel bad that Mr. Sims isn't doing so well. I just don't know how I can help. I mean Kevin and I aren't even together anymore." Gianna picked up a sweater, set the alarm and headed for the car.

Kevin pulled out the drive way and turned onto the street. Gianna watched as they drove past her house. Kevin turned on the radio and put his hand on hers. Gianna didn't move it. In fact it comforted her in some way. She was worried about Bryan. Charlene was still with Miles and they hadn't heard from him either.

"Don't worry Gianna, I am going to make this right." Kevin squeezed her hands and smiled at her. Gianna looked into sincere eyes with worry lines of concern etched around them. Gianna was in trouble because just looking at him, she could see that he meant every word. "Boy it only took his father on his death bed for him to get his shit together," Gianna thought to herself. Kevin's gesture did offer a bit of comfort and Gianna was able to relax and settle into the 3 hour ride to the Sims'

Mansion. "Plenty enough time to get the real deal out of him."

www.ingramcontent.com/pod-product-compliance
Lightning Source LLC
Chambersburg PA
CBHW071313130626
46556CB00004B/1589